LOOK BOOK

TANA HOBAN

Greenwillow Books, New York

Greenwillow Books, a division of
William Morrow & Company, Inc.,
1350 Avenue of the Americas,
New York, NY 10019.

Printed in Singapore by
Tien Wah Press
First Edition 10 9 8 7 6 5 4 3 2 1

LIBRARY OF CONGRESS
CATALOGING-IN-PUBLICATION DATA
Hoban, Tana.
Look book / by Tana Hoban.
    p.   cm.
Summary: Full-color nature photographs
are first viewed through a cut-out hole
and then in their entirety.
ISBN 0-688-14971-5 (trade).
ISBN 0-688-14972-3 (lib. bdg.)
1. Nature photography—Juvenile
literature.   2. Toy and movable books—
Specimens.   [1. Nature photography.
2. Photography.   3. Toy and movable
books.]   I. Title.   TR721.H6212 1997
779'.3—dc21   96-46268   CIP   AC

For Ava

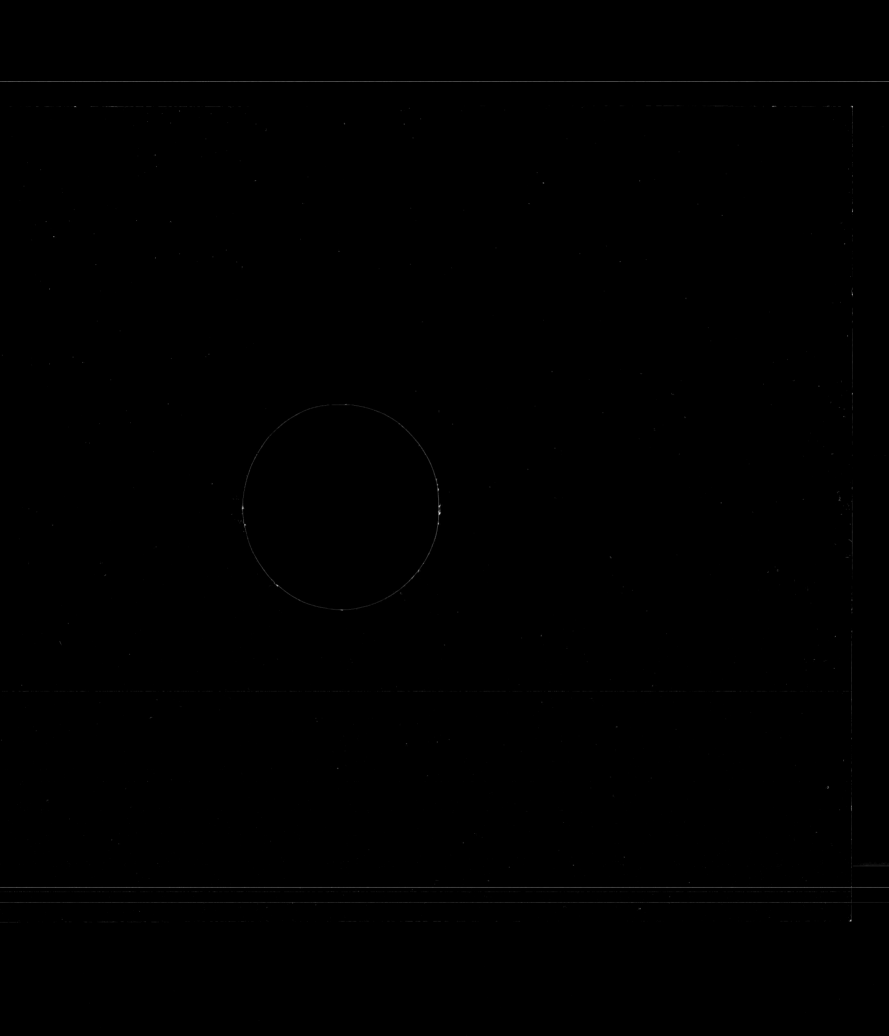

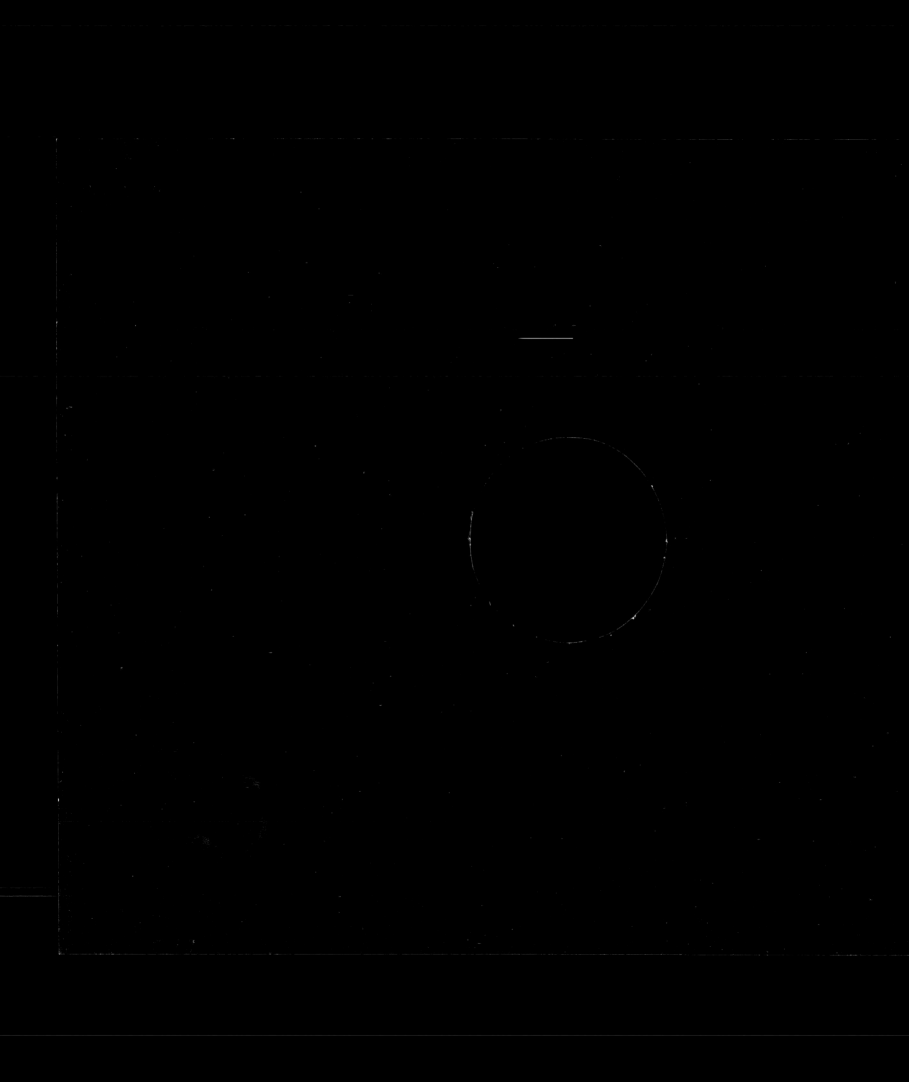

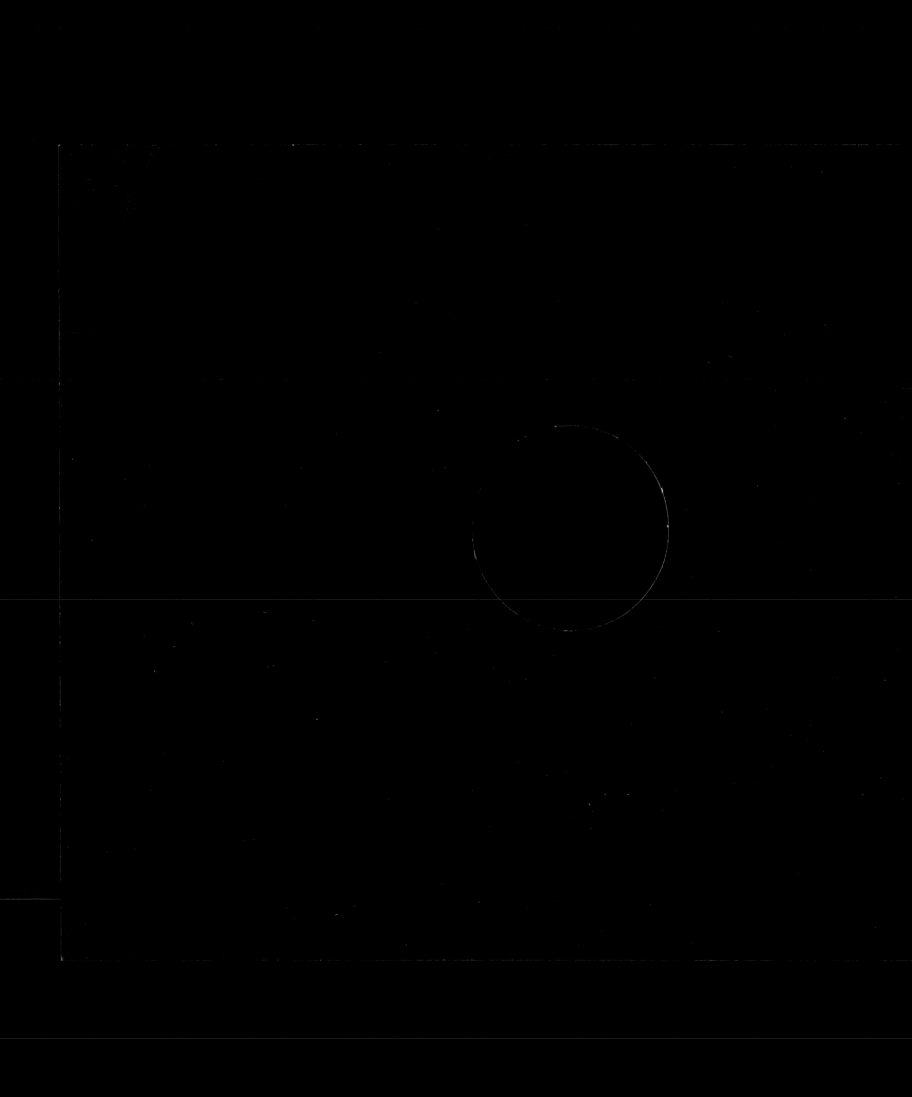

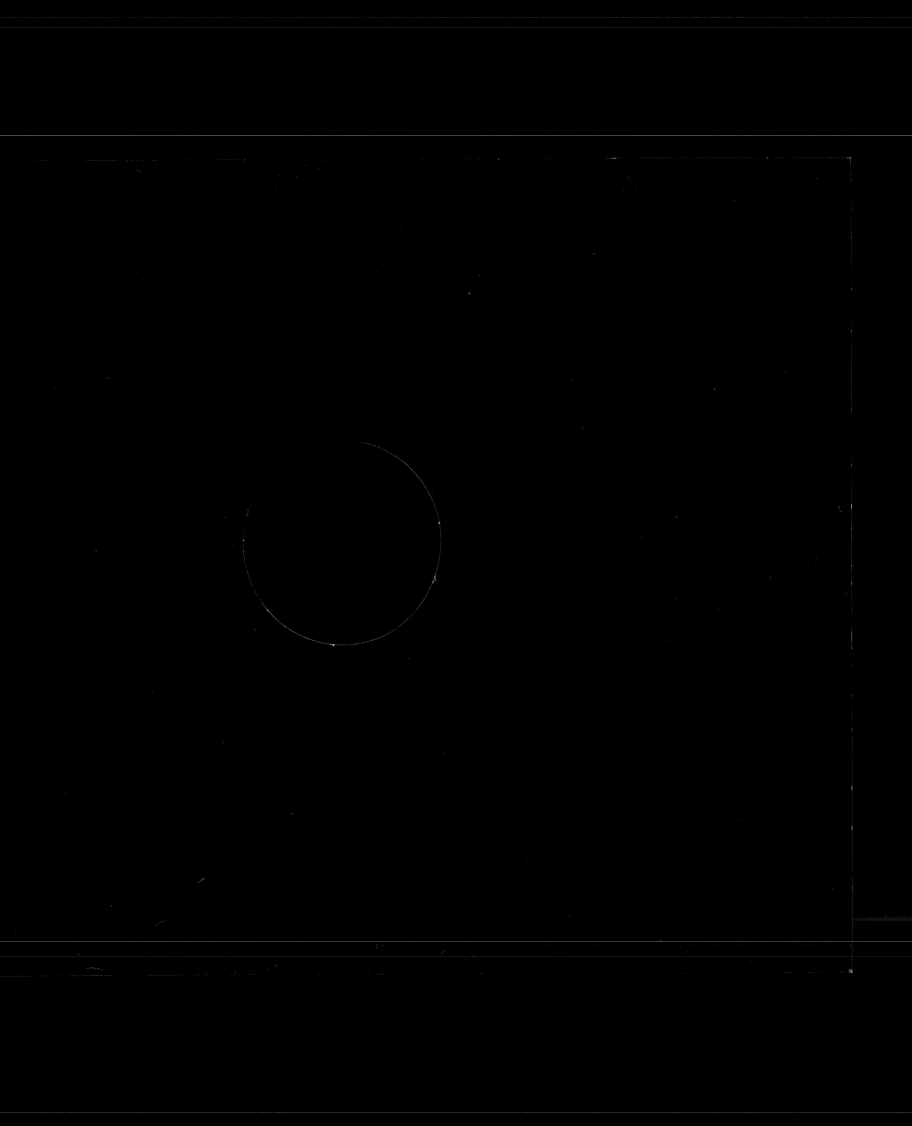

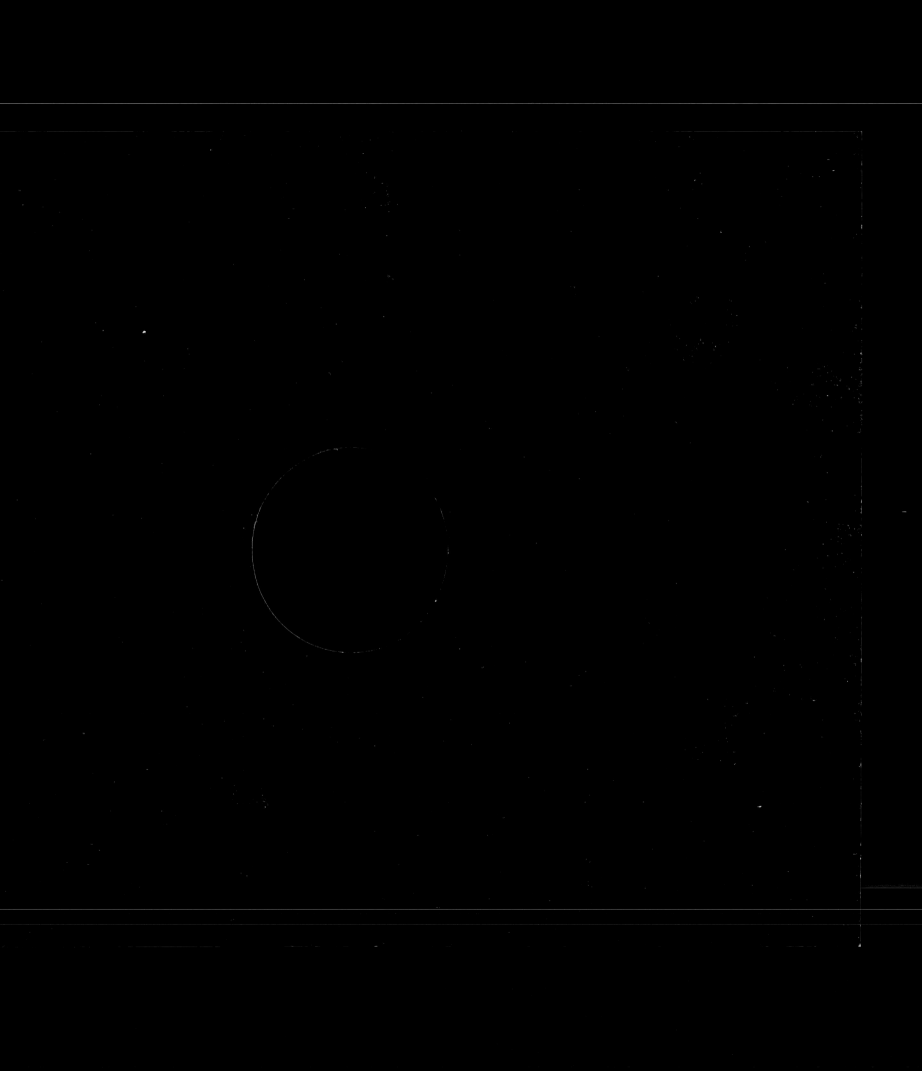

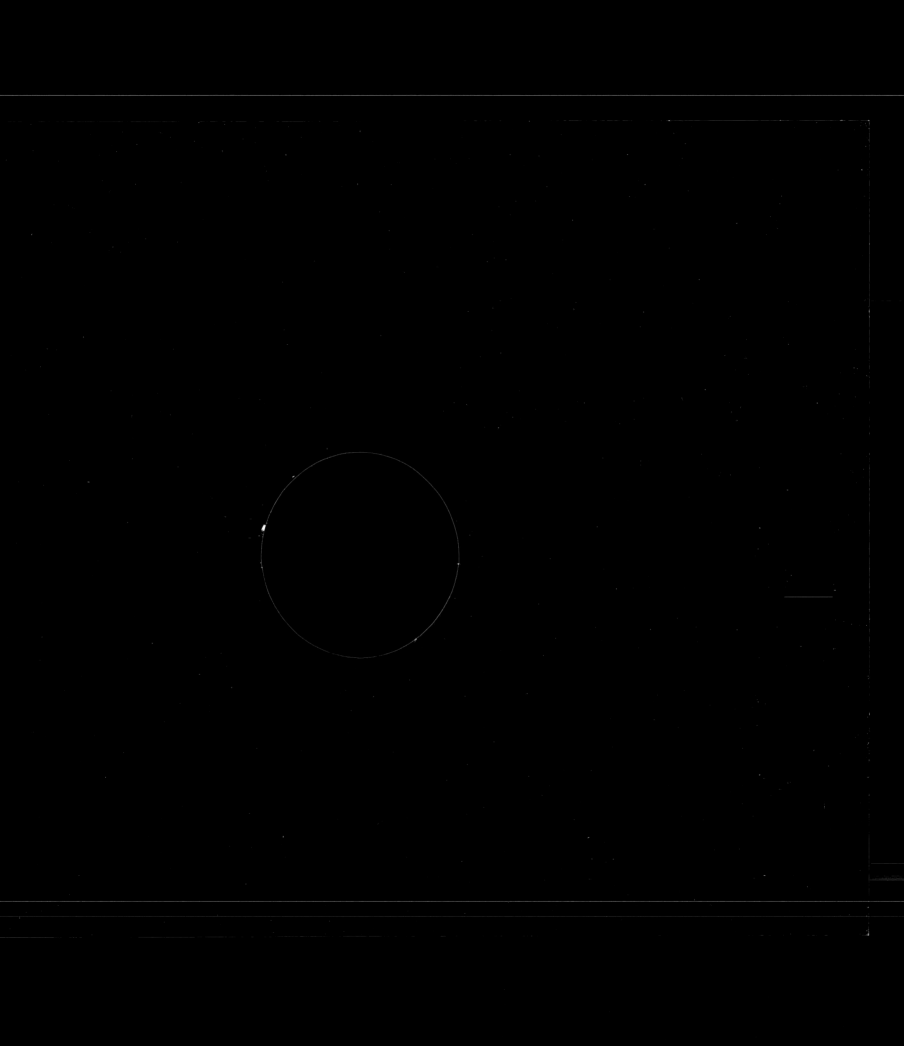

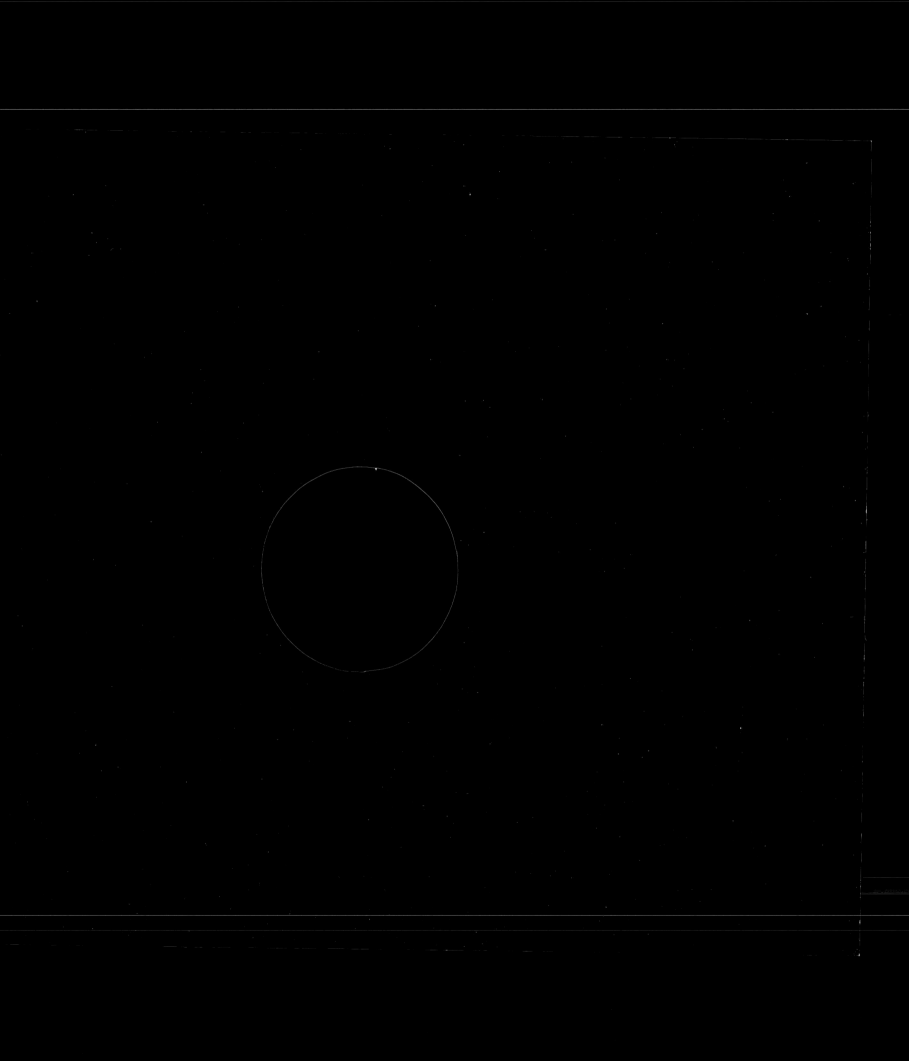

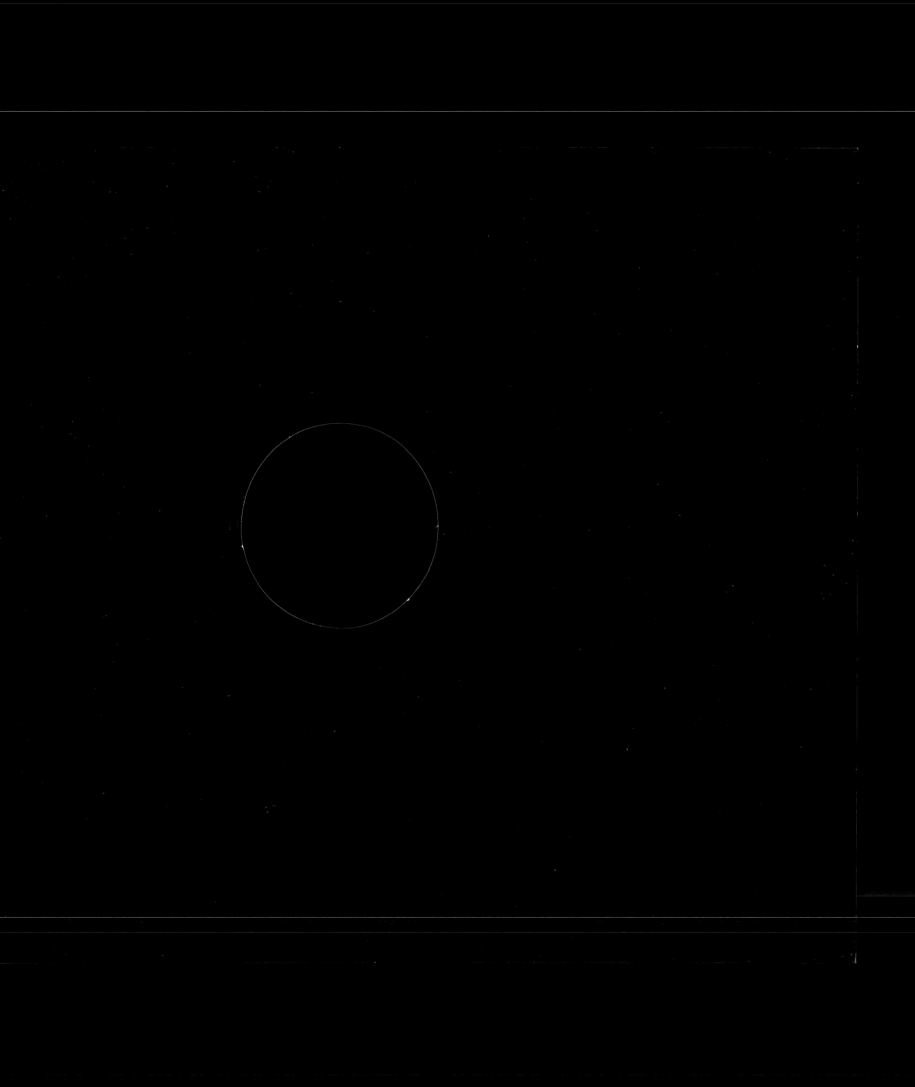

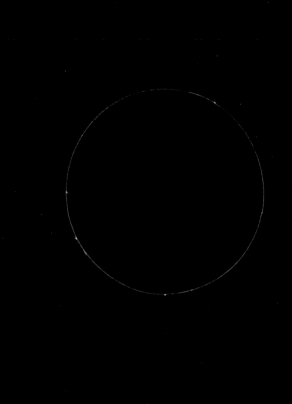

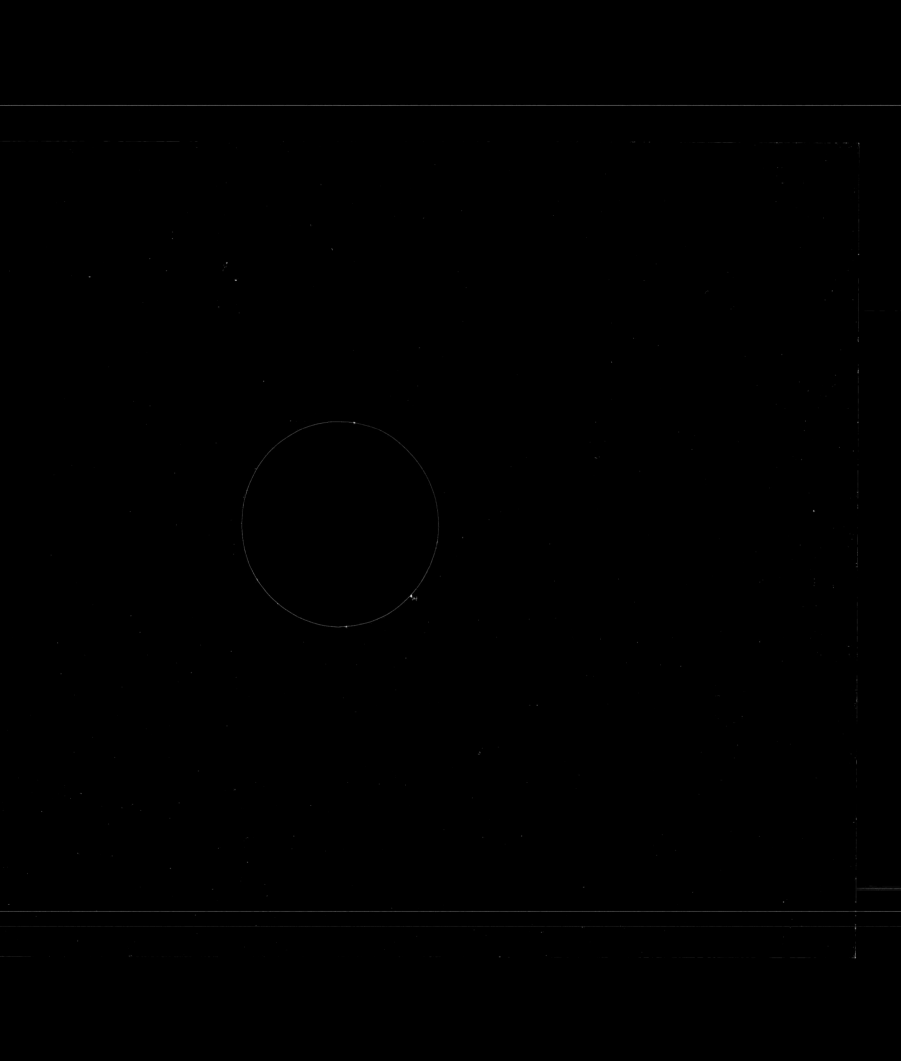

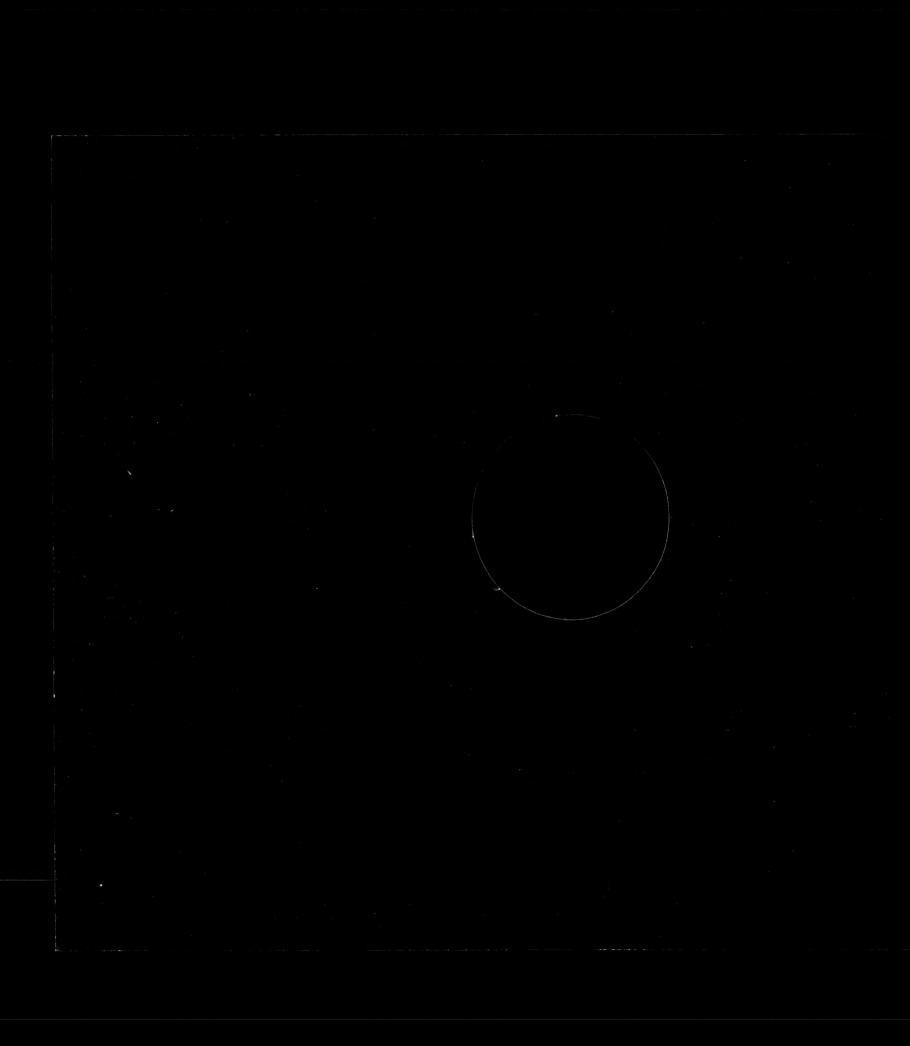